Arnie Lightning

THE THINGS I'M GRATEFUL FOR...

Arnie Lightning Books

Table of Contents

The Glad Game

Beth closed her book and sighed. Sometimes, it seemed strange to come back to real life after being lost between the pages of a good story for a couple of hours.

Right now, Beth was reading Pollyanna, the story of an orphaned little girl who went to live with her rich aunt after her parents died. Although her aunt wasn't the friendliest person, and although Pollyanna missed her parents very much, she still found something to be glad about every single day, no matter where she was or what she was doing. Pollyanna called this her "Glad Game."

Beth thought the Glad Game seemed like a very good idea. In her opinion, the world was too full of people who complained about what they didn't have, rather than acting thankful for the things they did have. Beth believed that if everyone were more like Pollyanna, the world would be a better place.

Beth stood up, stretched, and looked around. It was a bright, sunny afternoon, and the big tree Beth always sat under when she read cast a huge shadow over the grass beneath. It was getting toward the end of November, but you would never have guessed that from looking at Beth's big yard. Her southern California neighborhood stayed green and warm all year round.

Setting aside her Pollyanna book, Beth climbed onto her swing. It was a sturdy wooden swing on ropes that hung from a high, strong branch of the big, leafy tree. It was very special to Beth because her grandpa had made it for her when she was very little. Now, although her grandpa had passed away three years ago, Beth still thought of him whenever she swung.

As she pumped higher and higher, Beth stretched out her legs so that the tips of her toes seemed to touch the clouds in the sky. Her blonde ponytail swished behind her in the wind, and Beth thought, I'm really thankful for my swing. Even though Grandpa is gone now, he left me a memory that I'll keep forever.

Hey! Beth suddenly said to herself. I sound like Pollyanna playing the Glad Game! Maybe people still can do that! Maybe I'll teach my family!

Beth hopped off the swing in a burst of energy, picked up her book, and ran toward the house. Her brother Josh was sitting on the wide porch steps scowling down at his homework.

"I hate math!" he grumbled as Beth passed him.

Time to put the Glad Game into action! Beth thought happily. Turning to Josh, she smiled and said, "I know you hate math. Just think how good you'll feel when you're all done with school and you never have to do math again!"

"I can't wait," Josh replied. "It'll be a great feeling."

"It wouldn't feel so great, though, if you didn't already know how much you hated math," Beth pointed out. "So be glad you know!"

Josh stared at her, then shook his head. "You've got something there, squirt," he said.

Beth just smiled and went into the house. There, she found her teenage sister Angie sobbing inconsolably over the new at-home hair color she'd just tried out.

"It turned my hair orange!" she wailed. "I didn't want orange, I wanted strawberry-blonde!"

Beth gave her a hug. "You should be glad you still have your beautiful long hair," she said. "After all, a bad hair color is a lot easier to fix than a bad haircut."

Immediately, Angie stopped crying. "You're so right!" she exclaimed, brightening.

All throughout the days that followed, Beth did her best to be Pollyanna to her family and friends. Of course, there were times when she had to remind herself to play the Glad Game—like when her cat Misty ruined her favorite shirt. At first, Beth was really upset, but then she reasoned that she'd rather have Misty than have that old shirt, anyway!

When Dad got a flat tire on his car, Beth pointed out that he should be glad it went flat in the driveway rather than on the highway. And when Mom misplaced her favorite necklace and had to look for it for an hour, Beth was quick to remind her that she never would have found that scarf she'd lost a year ago if she hadn't lost her necklace too!

On Thanksgiving Day, as the family sat around the table to enjoy their pie and coffee, Dad lifted his mug and clinked it against Mom's. "I'd like to propose a toast," he announced. "To Beth!"

Beth's eyes widened in surprise. "Me?" she asked.

"Yes, you!" Dad went on. "Beth has been a little ray of sunshine to our family, teaching us to find the positive in everything we do."

Beth beamed. "It's called the Glad Game," she said.

"Yes, the Glad Game," smiled Mom.

Even Josh and Angie were beaming at Beth.

"And so in return," Dad concluded, "we'd like to remind our Beth how glad we are that she is in our lives!"

Beth was so happy, she could hardly speak. Warmth filled her heart and overflowed through her whole body. If the Glad Game can help my family so much, I'm sure it could do a ton for this world! she thought. Who knows? Maybe one day I'll be the gladdest President in the history of America!

Just for Fun Activity

Play your own version of the Glad Game! With a few friends or family members, spend some time cutting out pictures in old magazines that represent things you are glad about and grateful for. For example, you could cut out a picture of a dog to represent your own dog or a family to represent your own family. When everyone is finished cutting out their pictures, put them into an empty shoebox without looking at one another's pictures. Shake up the shoebox, and then take turns reaching in, pulling out pictures, and guessing who is grateful for what. Whoever guesses the most correctly gets to choose what's for dessert!

Everyday Blessings

Jack walked sadly through the forest, taking the shortcut home from school. Everyone at his old school had been nice to him, and Jack had had lots of friends there. But here in his new neighborhood, it was totally different.

Everyone Jack went to school with seemed to come from a well-to-do family. They wore nice clothes, and their parents picked them up in nice cars. They were always getting new things and comparing notes on the toys and games they did or didn't have yet. They didn't seem to know how to relate to Jack, and Jack certainly didn't know how to relate to them.

All of this made Jack feel very left-out. He and his family lived in a small, shabby house set far back from the road on an acre of overgrown land. Jack's parents were trying to clear the land and fix up the house in their spare time, but they both worked, and it was slow going.

Jack shared a small room with his three brothers. He didn't have a tablet or a phone like the kids at school did. He didn't even have an up-to-date video game system. And most of his clothes were hand-me-downs from his big brother Paul. His parents shared a car, and even the car had seen better days.

Jack sighed as he finally reached his yard. The moment he opened the gate to let himself in, his spotted dog Freckles rushed to meet him, barking and jumping excitedly.

Jack immediately forgot his bad mood. A grin stretched across his face, and he bent down to greet his pet. Freckles jumped into Jack's lap and licked his face. No matter what went on, Freckles was always in a good mood. He was Jack's best friend and the one bright spot Jack could count on every single day.

"Come on, Freckles!" called Jack, suddenly filled with fresh energy. Leaving his backpack by the front door, he broke into a run. "You can't catch me!" Jack yelled, laughing.

Freckles could never resist a good game of chase. He ran after Jack, his short spotted legs working overtime. Finally, Jack allowed Freckles to catch up to him. Breathless, the two of them fell into a heap at the foot of a sprawling oak tree.

The afternoon sun was warm, and Jack stretched out on his belly to rest. Freckles did the same. The breeze was soft on their faces, and the smell of grass and early-fall flowers filled their noses.

As they relaxed, Jack let his mind wander back to what had happened in class that day. His teacher, Mrs. Pearson, had announced that her students were going to start working on a thankfulness project. This project would focus on the everyday things that the students often took for granted and help them to be more appreciative of what they had.

After class, Jack had heard a lot of his classmates talking about what they were going to write about for their projects. One boy said that he was going to write about his brand-new mountain bike. A girl said that she was going to write about her family's upcoming trip to Hawaii.

Somehow, Jack didn't think that either of them had the right idea about this project. But then again, who was he to correct them? In the eyes of the kids at school, Jack didn't have a whole lot to be thankful for. And he had no idea what he was going to write about!

Jack's good mood began to fade—but then Freckles snuggled up closer to him, and Jack opened his eyes with a sudden inspiration.

Freckles! he thought. I'll write about my dog. After all, I think that's the sort of everyday thing Mrs. Pearson was talking about!

As the warm breeze continued to blow against his skin, Jack began to smile once more. A wonderful, loyal dog like Freckles and a big backyard where you can lie in the sun or run and explore or play for hours. The grass. The flowers. The blue sky and sunshine!

Before too long, Jack's mind and heart were overloaded with the everyday things in life that he always before taken for granted. Suddenly, he felt excited about doing this thankfulness project.

Maybe, just maybe, Jack said to himself, I'm not such a poor kid, after all!

Just for Fun Activity

Do you own thankfulness project! Make a big, long list of things you are thankful for. Be sure to list big and small things. Be thankful and appreciative of the things you have in your life!

Specially Different

Zoe lived with her grandparents and her cat Caterina in an ivy-covered red brick house at the edge of town.

Zoe had friends that she played with in the neighborhood. Some of them were true friends, and others were not. The ones who were not true friends talked behind Zoe's back. Zoe knew this because she had heard them from time to time, telling their other friends about her and how strange they thought she and her family were.

There was a long list of reasons that those kids made fun of Zoe, but none of them made sense to her.

So what if her grandmother was an eccentric retired artist who had painted every room in the house a different color, including the Summer Room, which was carpeted with fake grass and had its own sunshine-shaped light fixture? Who cared if Zoe's grandfather was a retired gourmet cook from France who spoke with a strong French accent and twirled his whiskers and bellowed opera songs at the top of his lungs?

Who cared if Zoe herself dressed according to her own individual style, preferring tie-dyed prints to plain ones and crazy wild curls to smooth, controlled ones? Who cared if Caterina was the only cat in the neighborhood who could meow in the tune of any television show theme song ever composed?

Zoe knew her family was different, but she thought their differences were wonderful and interesting. Where else could you go to sit in the sun on a blustery winter day besides the Summer Room? What other little girl in town got to eat crepe suzettes for breakfast besides Zoe? Who else had such fun putting together a creative wardrobe? And really, the fact that Caterina could practically sing made her one very talented cat in Zoe's eyes!

For all these reasons and then some, it didn't bother Zoe a bit what the other kids did or didn't think of her. She knew that her true friends would stick by her, no matter what. And as for the others, Zoe was smart enough to realize that the only reason they made fun of others was because they weren't very happy themselves. Knowing this, Zoe did her best to be nice to these not-so-loyal friends, even if they weren't very nice to her.

That was why she stopped riding her bike one fall afternoon when she spotted Allison, one of the girls who'd been making fun of Zoe behind her back, crying on the parkway near Zoe's house.

"Allison," Zoe asked hesitantly, "what's going on?"

Allison wiped her eyes. "Go away," she said in a tiny voice. "I'm fine."

Zoe did not believe that. "Come on, Allison," she urged. "You can tell me the truth. Then maybe I can help you."

"Why would you want to do that?" asked Allison. "Why are you being so nice to me, Zoe? I know you've heard me say some not-so-nice things about you and your family."

"That's true," Zoe told her. "But that doesn't mean I don't care about you. So, what's wrong?"

Allison sighed. Finally, she said, "My mom is working late tonight, and my dad is out of town. My sister went to sleep over at a friend's house, and I forgot to take the spare key to school with me this morning. Now I can't get into my house till my mom gets back, and that'll be after dark. I've already tried calling some of my friends, but they're not picking up and—"

Zoe didn't need to hear anymore. "Come with me, Allison," she said. "Let's go back to my house and leave a message with your mom. Then you can hang out with us till she comes home."

Allison's mouth gaped. "Are you sure you want me to?" she asked guiltily.

"Don't be silly!" answered Zoe.

And so the two girls went back to Zoe's house and left a message with Allison's mom, letting her know where she was. Then they spent the rest of the afternoon studying in the Summer Room.

"I'd heard about the Summer Room, but never seen it!" Allison exclaimed. "It's beautiful, Zoe!"

Zoe grinned. Soon, the two girls were laughing and talking their way through their homework.

For dinner, Zoe's grandfather made filet mignons in the shape of hearts, with delicious, creamy crème brulee for dessert.

Afterward, Zoe's grandmother spent a little while teaching both girls how to splatter-paint.

And the whole time they worked, Caterina keep them energized with the theme songs from all their favorite TV shows.

By the time Allison's mom came to pick her up, Allison was sad to leave. She turned to Zoe and gave her a big hug. "I'm so sorry I ever made fun of you and your family," she said. "You guys are different, but your differences are what make you so much fun, and so special. You really have a lot to be grateful for Zoe!"

Zoe returned Allison's hug. "I really do, don't I?" she cried.

Just for Fun Activity

Just like Zoe, everyone is unique in his or her own special way. Design a poster to hang on the door of your room that is uniquely you. Choose your favorite color of poster board. Write "______'s Room" in large letters in the center (insert your name in the ______)

Now comes the fun part—adding details that truly reflect you. Decorate the poster board with your favorite photographs, stickers, souvenirs (like ticket stubs, play programs, etc.), and more. Add a dash of glitter, confetti, mini beads, feathers, sports cards, pom-poms, or anything else that is uniquely you and will give your craft a special touch. Finally, let the glue dry and hang the poster on the door of your room! After all, it's uniquely yours!!

Tropical Thanksgiving

"When will the leaves change color?" Evan asked his parents. He and his family had just moved to Florida from Michigan that past summer, and as far as Evan could tell, autumn was taking an awfully long time to arrive.

Evan's mom laughed, putting a jar of jelly on the breakfast table. "Oh, Evan, honey, we're in Florida," she said.

Evan stared at her. "So?"

"So," his dad said gently, "in Florida, it stays green and sunny and warm all year round. The leaves on the trees don't change colors. It's just like summer all the time!"

Evan's parents seemed to think this was great news—but Evan was horrified. "You mean, there are no leaf piles to jump in—ever? No snow at Christmastime? No shiny icicles hanging above the windows in the winter?"

Mom handed Evan a piece of toast with jelly on it. "That's right," she answered gently. "It's very different here than it was in Michigan."

"I don't like it!" protested Evan. Suddenly, he wasn't very hungry for his breakfast. "I want to move back to Michigan!"

"Don't be silly!" said his dad. "Wait till you hear what your mom and I have planned for Thanksgiving."

"Thanksgiving?" asked Evan. "Is that coming up soon?"

"Yes," smiled his mom. "Next week, in fact. Your dad and I have decided to rent a big boat from the marina and have Thanksgiving dinner on the water with some of our friends and coworkers. Won't that be fun?"

Evan was even more upset now. To him, Thanksgiving was all about a cozy, warm holiday when he and his parents gathered with their extended family for a huge turkey dinner at Grandma and Grandpa Wyatt's house. There was always a fire in the fireplace, frost on the windows, and a blustery wind outside.

Here in Florida, Evan felt a million miles removed from all of that. Florida was not cozy at all. If you built a fire here, you would roast. There was no such thing as frost in this part of the country. Even the wind here was warm!

Evan did not think that spending Thanksgiving on a boat would be fun at all! Who had ever heard of something as silly as that?

One week later, Evan was standing in the hot sun on the deck of the boat his parents had rented for the occasion. The smell of turkey wafted over from the grill his dad had set up on the deck, and Evan knew that inside the cabin of the boat, there was a huge spread of pies, casseroles, and other side dishes.

The kids of Evan's parents' coworkers ran wild around the deck, laughing and calling to each other. When the boat pulled to a stop, they hollered happily.

"Can we jump in the water and go swimming?" a girl eagerly asked her mother.

"Sure, Emma," her mom replied, smiling. "But stay close to the boat. We'll be having our Thanksgiving dinner in less than an hour."

When the other kids heard her say this, they all began splashing off the boat into the Gulf of Mexico. All except Evan—and Emma.

"Evan?" Emma asked softly. "Aren't you coming swimming with us?"

Evan scowled at her. "Go in without me," he said. "It was your idea."

Emma looked unhappy. "I don't know why you're so sad," she said. "Is it because you miss your old home? I've moved before, and I know it's hard. But—"

Evan cut her off. "This is a lousy Thanksgiving!" he cried, folding his arms stubbornly. "Who ever heard of Thanksgiving on a boat in the middle of the Gulf of Mexico, with turkey on the grill, and kids going swimming, and sunshine, and seagulls, and—"

It was Emma's turn to interrupt him. "Listen to yourself!" she exclaimed. "Doesn't that sound like most people's idea of a dream Thanksgiving?"

Evan was caught off-guard. He realized suddenly that Emma was right. "I... guess...so," he admitted slowly.

Emma smiled. "Silly," she told him. "Come on, let's go swimming."

Before Evan knew what he was doing, he was jumping into the water right behind Emma. Without even meaning to, he began to have the time of his life, splashing and playing with the other kids.

He couldn't believe how fast the time went! As quick as wink, it was time to eat dinner. And, as Evan sat at the table on the deck of the boat with his parents and their friends, he realized suddenly that although Florida wasn't much like Michigan, that wasn't necessarily a bad thing.

Summer all year, Evan thought to himself with a smile. And Thanksgiving on a boat! Now that's something to be thankful for!

A Special Sundae

"Mom!" whined Kai. "Why didn't you get Triple-Cherry-Chocolate Crunch Balls?"

Kai and his mom were grocery shopping. They had just walked right past the cereal aisle—and yet Mom had not put a box of Kai's favorite cereal in the cart.

Mom sighed. "Last time I bought you that, Kai," she said, "you let half the box go stale!"

Kai folded his arms and pouted. His mom could be so unfair. But before he could think too long and hard about that, Kai spotted a display that immediately caught his eye.

"Mooom!" he cried. "Look at that! They have chocolate-chip cookies shaped like Captain Moonstar." Captain Moonstar was Kai's favorite cartoon character. He was a superhero who lived in outer space and came to earth on live-saving missions.

Mom sighed again. "We already have cookies in the house, Kai. We don't need any shaped like Captain Moonstar."

"But, Mom!" Kai started to protest. That was when he spotted a big display of boxes holding little Christmas houses made entirely of chocolate! The holidays hadn't even begun yet, but these were just the sort of thing stores put out to get their customers interested ahead of time.

"Oh my gosh, Mom!" cried Kai. "We have to get a chocolate house! We could put a chocolate-chip Captain Moonstar inside—but only if you let me get a box of those too! And then we could—"

"Kai David Kishi!" Mom interrupted. "We are not getting those cookies, and we are not getting a chocolate house, and that is final. If you're going to keep begging me to buy everything you see, then maybe I'll just have to leave you at home next time I go to the grocery store."

Kai pouted again. "No fair!" he said as they neared the checkout counter. "I'm the only kid in the world who doesn't get to have fun food like that."

"Think again," Mom replied, pointing to a sign above a large bin just inside the exit doors.

While Mom unloaded her purchases onto the conveyor belt, Kai curiously pushed past her and walked right up to the bin. The sign above it read, "Donate boxed, bagged, or canned food items for residents of Cherry Valley Shelter for the Homeless. Give the less fortunate a Thanksgiving dinner they'll never forget!"

Kai studied the pictures that decorated the sign. There were a few of adults, but there were also several of kids who were around his age. They were smiling happily as they sat at a table and ate pumpkin pie piled with fluffy whipped cream.

The caption under the pictures read, "Last year's Thanksgiving feast, made possible by the generous donations of people like you!"

Kai gasped. He hadn't known that Cherry Valley had a homeless shelter, or that the kids who lived in those places had to depend on other people (besides their own parents) to supply them with food and a little bit of holiday fun.

Suddenly, Kai felt very guilty for the way he'd begged for everything he saw and whined and complained to Mom. Who was he to complain when there were kids just a few miles away who didn't even have houses, let alone much in the way of food?

When Mom came out of the checkout line, she headed straight for Kai. "I see you checked out the sign," she told him, smiling. "Would you like to put this mashed-potato mix and these cans of vegetables into the bin?"

She handed Kai a few of her own purchases, and he added them to the growing pile of food items inside the bin.

As he and Mom headed out of the store, Kai said to her, "I'm sorry, Mom. I guess I wasn't acting very grateful earlier."

Mom smiled and put her hand on his shoulder. "You do have a lot to be grateful for," she agreed.

That night after dinner, Mom fixed Kai an enormous ice cream sundae for a special treat. It was piled with whipped cream, sprinkles, and a couple of sugar wafers.

Kai admired the sundae for a moment just before he dug in. Tomorrow, he thought to himself, I'll see what I can do about making sure the kids at Cherry Valley Shelter for the Homeless have ice cream to go with their pie!

Maze 1

Maze 2

Maze 3

Maze 4

Maze 5

Maze 6

Maze 7

Maze 8

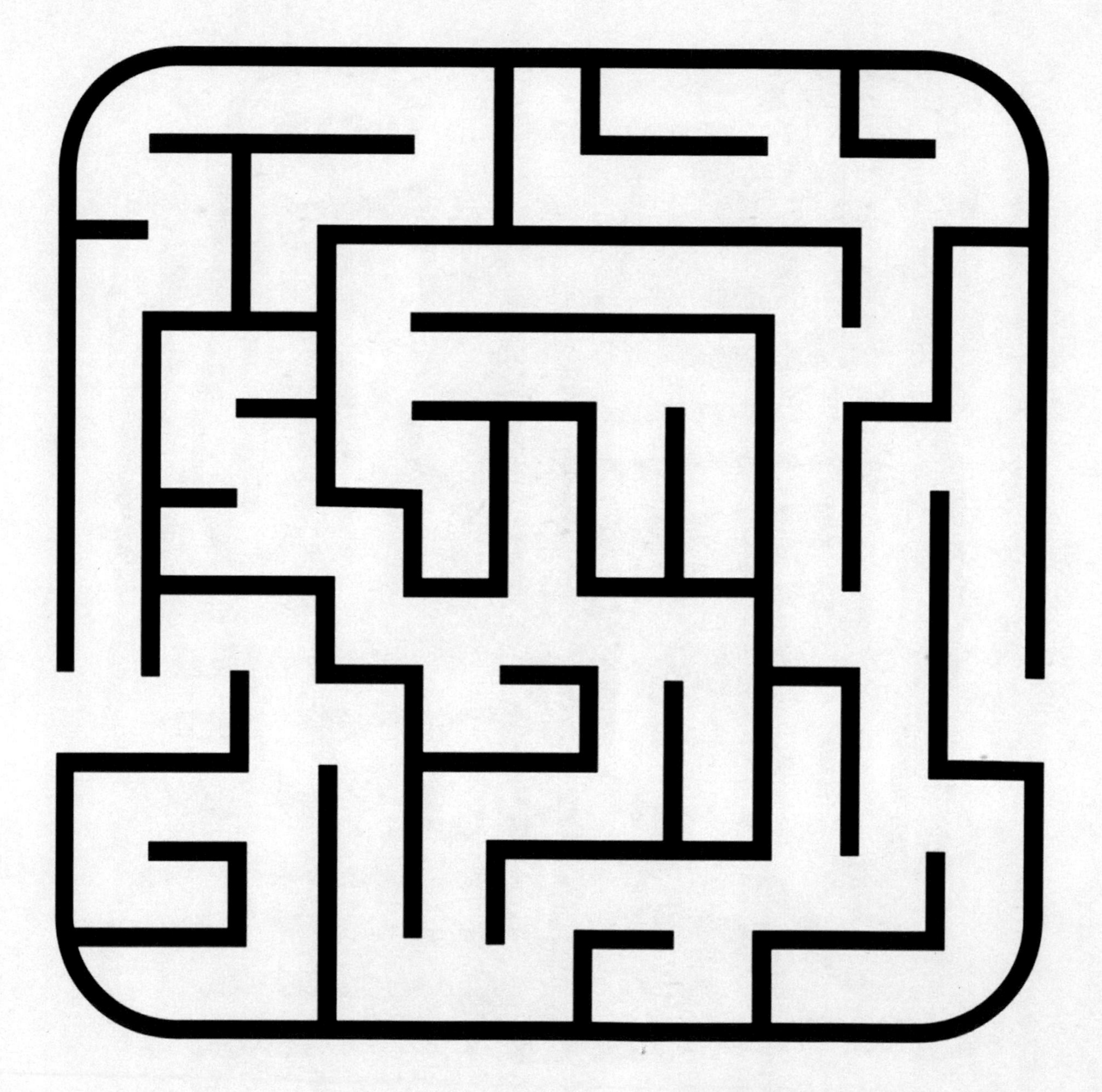

Maze Solutions

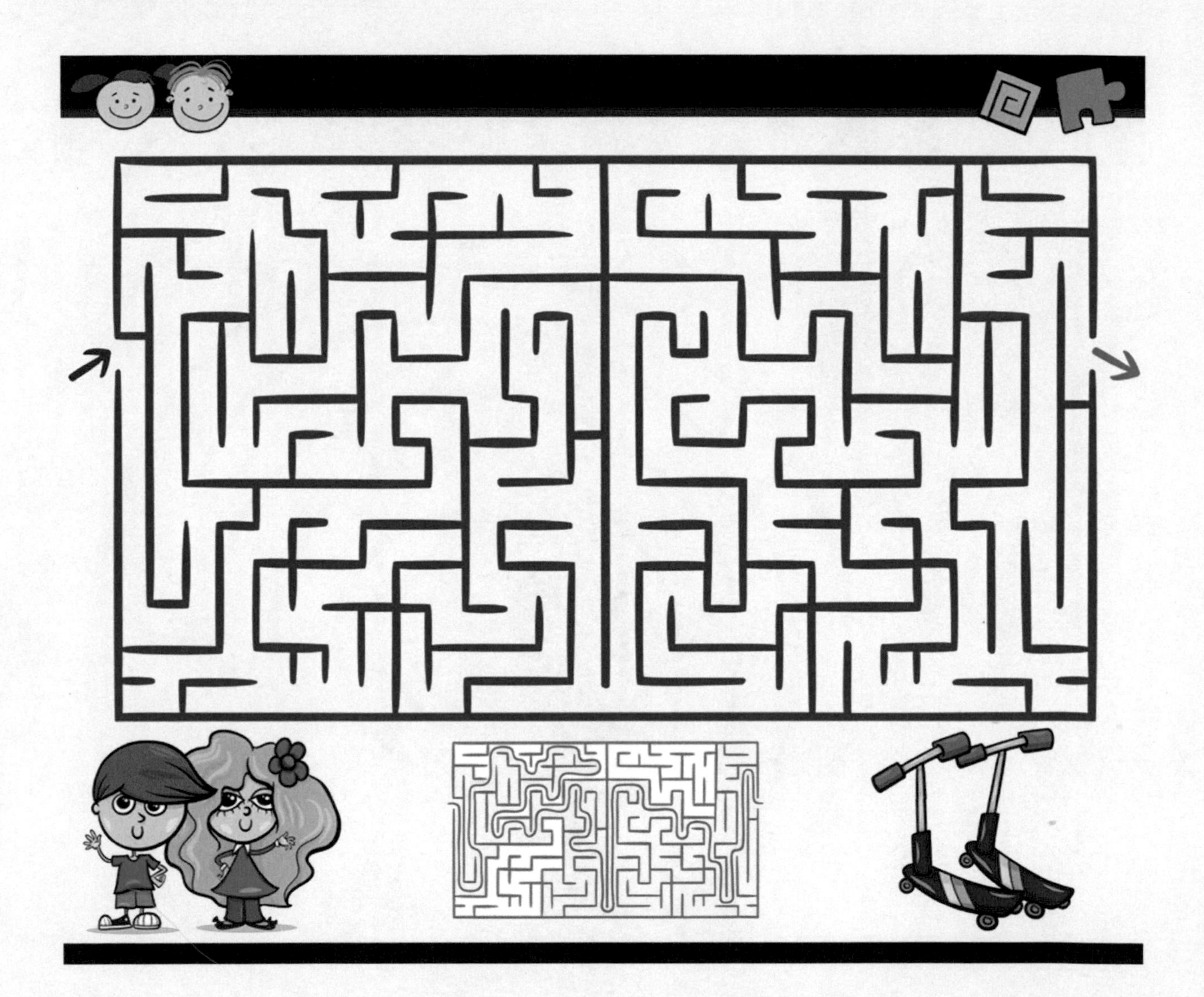

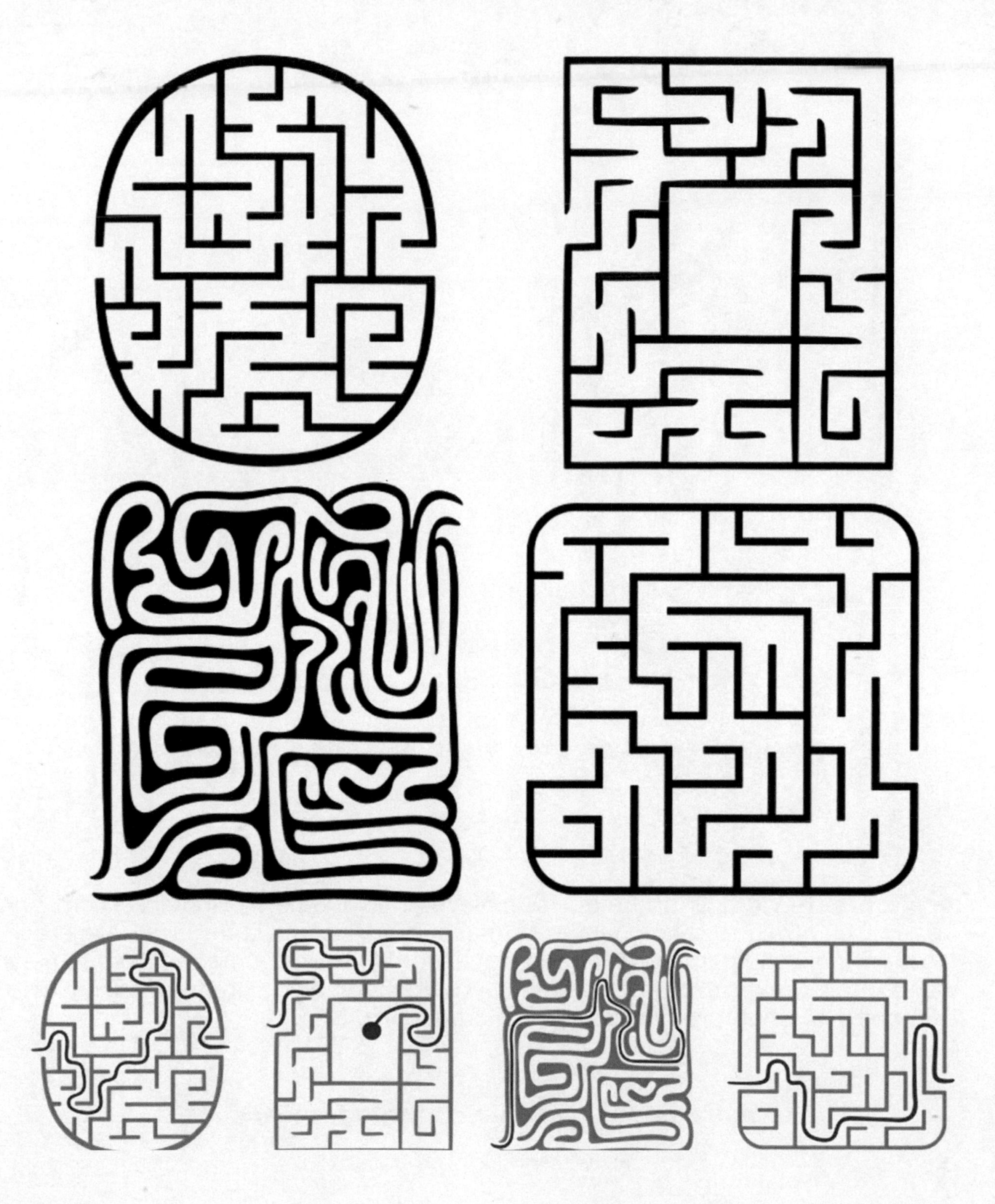

About the Author

Arnie Lightning is a dreamer. He believes that everyone should dream big and not be afraid to take chances to make their dreams come true. Arnie enjoys writing, reading, doodling, and traveling. In his free time, he likes to play video games and run. Arnie lives in Mississippi where he graduated from The University of Southern Mississippi in Hattiesburg, MS.

For more books by Arnie Lightning, please visit:

www.ArnieLightning.com

42320306R00020

Made in the USA
San Bernardino, CA
30 November 2016